ONCE UPON
A TIME

CUMB...

Edited by Allie Jones

First published in Great Britain in 2015 by:

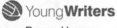

Remus House
Coltsfoot Drive
Peterborough
PE2 9BF
Telephone: 01733 890066
Website: www.youngwriters.co.uk

All Rights Reserved
Book Design by **ASHLEY JANSON**
© Copyright Contributors 2015
SB ISBN 978-1-78443-537-0

Printed and bound in the UK by BookPrintingUK
Website: www.bookprintinguk.com

FOREWORD

Welcome, Reader!

For Young Writers' latest competition, **Once Upon A Time**, we gave school children nationwide the tricky challenge of writing a story with a beginning, middle and an end in just 100 words, and they rose to the challenge magnificently!

We chose stories for publication based on style, expression, imagination and technical skill. The result is this entertaining collection full of diverse and imaginative mini sagas, which is also a delightful keepsake to look back on in years to come.

Here at Young Writers our aim is to encourage creativity in children and to inspire a love of the written word, so it's great to get such an amazing response, with some absolutely fantastic stories. This made it a tough challenge to pick the winners, so well done to Ross who has been chosen as the best author in this anthology. You can see the winning story on the front cover.

I'd like to congratulate all the young authors in Once Upon A Time - Cumbria - I hope this inspires them to continue with their creative writing. And who knows, maybe we'll be seeing their names on the best seller lists in the future...

Jenni Bannister

Editorial Manager

CONTENTS

AMBLESIDE CE PRIMARY SCHOOL, AMBLESIDE

Alex Jackson (10) 1
Joshua Lassey (9) 2
Peony Chen (9) 3
Bethan Rowley (11) 4
Robert Porter (9) 5
Jack Cunnningham (11) 6
Giselle Meschino (10) 7
Sadie Irving (10) 8

BOWNESS-ON-SOLWAY PRIMARY SCHOOL, WIGTON

Tom Blackledge (9) 9
Evelyn Twigg (9) 10
Annabelle Wills (10) 11
James Paisley 12
Jack Sadler (10) 13
Joe Irving (11) 14
Lana Twigg (8) 15
Ellie Sheather (9) 16
Kane Whitehead (9) 17
Kirsty Castles (9) 18
Jonathan Wills (8) 19

CAMBRIDGE PRIMARY SCHOOL, BARROW-IN-FURNESS

Keira Louise Walker (9) 20
Alan Falloon (8) 21
Imogen Ashton (8) 22
Breeanna Corkill (8) 23
Leanne Southward (8) 24
Jake Holmes (9) 25
Elise Olga Charnley (8) 26
Kate Hardman (9) 27
Richard Bown (8) 28
Logan Garner (8) 29
Stephanie Marie Carter (9) 30
Kingsley Craig (9) 31
Brooke Alderson (8) 32

GRANGE CE PRIMARY SCHOOL, GRANGE-OVER-SANDS

Kacey Procter (8) 33
Alice Walmsley (7) 34
Ross Best (8) 35
Diya Elizabeth Biju Chempananikel (8) 36
Erin Hathorn (7) 37
Leo Michael Macdonald (7) 38
William Morrell (7) 39
Isaac Johnston (7) 40
Jayden Latham Saunders (7) 41
Samuel Jackson (8) 42
Dan Phillips (8) 43
Alfie Boydell (7) 44
Thomas Mallinson (7) 45
Matthew Barker (10) 46
Cameron Barnsley (8) 47
Leila Higgins (8) 48
Samuel Herrema (9) 49
Amelie Taylor (8) 50
Jayden James Reading (9) 51
Kira McLaughlin (9) 52
Evie Dobson (10) 53
Joe Taylor (10) 54
Herbie Harrison (10) 55
Grace Davis (9) 56
Mia Best (10) 57
Ross (10) 58
Daisy McLaughlin (6) 59
Emily Williams (7) 60
Sean Kerr (6) 61
Caleb Higgins (6) 62
Skye Scholey (9) 63
Alex Otway (9) 64
Thomas Ashley (9) 65
Gemma Lacey (9) 66
Tom Agliolo (9) 67
Idris Illingworth (7) 68
Patrycja Polec (6) 69
Vincent Lacey (6) 70

Roshana Joy Higginson (6) 71
Paige McLaughlin (6).......................... 72
Heather Lowes (7) 73
Mary Phoebe Dobson (8) 74
Sophia Elle Maher (8).......................... 75
Jayden Lewis Buchan (9) 76
Ryelainn Scholey (8) 77
Jack Williams (8) 78

ST HERBERT'S CE PRIMARY & NURSERY SCHOOL, KESWICK

Hilton Yener Etisoy (8) 79
Thomas Price 80
Oliver Pepper....................................... 81
Ebony Sienna Heels (8)........................ 82
Lauren Emily Garty (7) 83
Dylan Speight (8)................................. 84

ST MARGARET MARY CATHOLIC PRIMARY SCHOOL, CARLISLE

Charlotte Andrews (10).......................... 85
Emily Taylor (10).................................. 86
Ruby Perrett (8) 87
Amelia Dixon (5) 88
Ruby Grace Henry (9) 89
Heather Christina Amot (9) 90
Nadine Thomlinson (9) 91
Freya Ackley (9)................................... 92
Shannon White (9)................................ 93
Joe Armstrong (10) 94
Jake Robinson (10) 95
Sonny Hull (9)...................................... 96
Molly Emily Craig (7) 97
Ellis Patrick John Lavery (10) 98
Neo Storey (9) 99
Charlie Taylor (9) 100
Connor Briggs (9) 101
Dylan Hull (10).................................... 102
Mikey Waugh (10) 103
Kelsey-Lea Clark (11) 104

SCOTBY CE PRIMARY SCHOOL, CARLISLE

Megan Bunting (8) 105
Eva Carthy (8) 106
Jamie Longrigg (9)............................... 107

Katie Blenkinsopp (8) 108
Ellis Beattie (9) 109
Daria Nik (9) 110
Sarah-Jane Cochrane (8)......................111
Caitlan Osgood (10) 112
Jessica Anthony (9) 113
Sam Glencross (8)................................114
Oliver Kennedy (9)................................115
Charlotte Bell (9)..................................116
Olivia Robertson (10)............................117
Holly Robins (9)....................................118
Joseph Grayson (9) 119
Poppi Bowe (9) 120
Joel McCormick (7)............................. 121
Matthew Bell (7).................................. 122
Rae Platton (7) 123
Rosie Cairns (7).................................. 124
Cerys Richardson (7)........................... 125
Dylan Nettleship (7) 126
Ella Smith (7) 127
Ethan Bell (7)...................................... 128
Jasmine Murray (7).............................. 129
Petrina Walker (10) 130
Charlie Lomas 131
Sam Jamieson (10) 132
Liam Robinson (10) 133
Robyn Bainbridge (11)......................... 134
Jacob Platton (11)............................... 135
Leah Barnes (10)................................. 136
Ellie Swift (10)..................................... 137
Finlay Barraclough (9) 138
Eve Cogan (9) 139
Abbie Kenny (10)................................. 140
Sophie Irving (9).................................. 141
Matthew Walker Scott (11).................... 142
Maddie Wildridge (10) 143

THE BISHOP HARVEY GOODWIN SCHOOL (CHURCH OF ENGLAND VOLUNTARY AIDED), CARLISLE

Keira Perrett (10)................................. 144
Kyle McNeill (10) 145
Maisie Little (10) 146
Candice O'Neil (9) 147
Ellie Troughton (9) 148

Melissa Russell (10) 149
Oliver Jessiman (11) 150
Rebecca Bevins (10) 151
Travis Bennett (9) 152
Ethan Nicholson (10) 153
Jacob Callaghan (10) 154

WINDERMERE PREPARATORY SCHOOL, WINDERMERE

Serena Cooper (8) 155
Hector Westmoreland Nicholson (8) 156
Josh Done (8) 157
Emma Heginbotham (9) 158
Eva Baker (8) 159
Charlie Hodson (8) 160
Cristian Waddell Lallana (8) 161
Clarissa Cooper (9) 162
Elizabeth Kaye (8) 163
Bethany Saunders (9) 164
Katie Holgate (8) 165
Hamish Ross (8) 166
Eddie Lewis (8) 167
Taya Wade-Wilson (8) 168
Tom Johnson (8) 169
Felix Hugo Stewart (7) 170
Harriet Read (7) 171
Patia May Pickering (8) 172
Nuala Sankey (8) 173
Millie Westmoreland Nicholson (7) 174
Jake Harris (8) 175
Ranulph Turton (7) 176
Tom Johnson (8) 177

THE
MINI SAGAS

World Cup Dream

There lived a boy who loved football. He played in the park every day, and dreamt of playing in a World Cup. He played for his local team, Ambleside, and played every Saturday. He was spotted by a scout and went to play at an academy, and played against big teams but still dreamt of playing for his country when he was older. Then one day he got the chance to play for a top team, his dream was getting closer. He then got to play for his country, and scored the winning goal! Who said dreams can't come true?

Alex Jackson (10)
Ambleside CE Primary School, Ambleside

Dark And Light

One night I couldn't sleep, then I saw a light coming from the back garden. I looked through the window, there was light. When I looked closer it had yellow eyes. But when I looked in the dark corner, I saw evil-looking ones, then they started to chase the yellow one. I leaned out but when I did the evil one took a step back. I then realised that it was my good luck charm, so I threw it down. Suddenly they vanished. After that the yellow one lived with me. I called him Sparky.

Joshua Lassey (9)
Ambleside CE Primary School, Ambleside

Christmas Fairy Magic

'Oh no, I've burnt the chicken. What will my parents think when they get here?'

Meanwhile the fairies had been watching... She went to tell Harry the news and they flew in and unburnt it. Harry said, 'What are you talking about? It's not burnt at all!'

'Help! The best bauble has broken.' So she went to tell Harry.

'It's all in one piece,' he said.

'But how? Maybe I imagined it, I think I'm just tired.'

In the end they all had a successful Christmas. The best was the chicken! The fairies flew home to practise more magic spells.

Peony Chen (9)
Ambleside CE Primary School, Ambleside

Cinderella And The Not So Charming Prince

Having lived happily with the prince, Cinderella was devastated to overhear what he was saying. 'I only married that rat of a girl so I could commit crimes without being discovered,' he said. 'Cinderella would you like to go to the jewellery shop?' But she knew what was coming.

Once they arrived he blew up most of the town. *Why?* she thought, *he is a prince?* Cinderella was imprisoned, but he escaped! Eventually they found out that he was, a villain, which meant she was released. Unfortunately they never caught the 'prince', he might still be out there.

Bethan Rowley (11)
Ambleside CE Primary School, Ambleside

4

Beware Of Learner Fairies

High above the village of Kahuna, lived an ordinary, dull, Herdwick sheep called Barbara, who always wanted to be special. She rescued a fairy from a dry stone wall. The fairy granted her three wishes. The first wish was to be pink, but surprisingly she ended up brown. Her second wish to be able to jump higher than the other sheep, but she could only hop. Confused and furious, the third wish was to be normal. She thought she was OK, so she let out a happy moo. Only then did she notice the L plate on the fairy's back...

Robert Porter (9)
Ambleside CE Primary School, Ambleside

Jack And Harry And The Xbox Time Machine

Once upon a time there were two boys called Jack and Harry, who had an Xbox time machine. They decided to go back to the dinosaur age. When they got there they saw lots and lots of dinosaurs, but one was the meanest dinosaur, it was a T-rex. So Jack and Harry ran for their lives. They had to run for a day and found a cave, and hid inside. When it was safe Jack and Harry still had the time machine, and they went back to the year 2014.

Jack Cunnningham (11)
Ambleside CE Primary School, Ambleside

Trans Tower

Bumblebee and Grimlock had been recruited by Optimus Prime to destroy Death Moon, who was trying to take over the world by using the Eiffel Tower. Death Moon was standing at the top and Bumblebee was climbing up. He reached the top in a struggle, and way behind him was Grimlock. When Bumblebee was fighting they sliced through the Eiffel Tower, and made him wake, which caused Grimlock, who was still climbing, to fall off. Suddenly Ratchet (their doctor) appeared and rescued him. The tower, with help from Bumblebee, turned on Death Moon and killed him. The mission was complete.

Giselle Meschino (10)
Ambleside CE Primary School, Ambleside

Seven Dancers

'Sadie, come on, dance time.' So she met her friends, they were called Maddie, Mackenzie, Kendal, Nia, Chloe and Paige. They had a competition to do so they came out of the dressing room to dance. They learnt their dance in five days. There was a competition and Maddie had a solo, so she was getting ready to go on, but she forgot it! It was her turn to go, so she danced, but forgot her steps and she ran off stage crying...

Sadie Irving (10)
Ambleside CE Primary School, Ambleside

Why Monkeys Eat Bananas

Once, there was a monkey who was called Bob. He was swinging through trees, eating cookies. He thought to himself: *Cookies are kind of old; I should move on to oranges or cakes. Or even broccoli!*

Days passed and he was wondering about food stuff. Cauliflower, cakes, spinach and so on. Soon he was getting sick of cookies. He thought desperately, then he thought: *Bananas!* So soon he was swinging through the trees with his friends, and they were eating the new craze. Every single monkey in the whole universe! Bob was really happy to be top monkey! Hooray!

Tom Blackledge (9)
Bowness-on-Solway Primary School, Wigton

Lost And Found

I woke up and realised my dragon egg was missing. I had my breakfast and was now in the forest with my sister Emelia and Reuben, our dog. 'What was that Emelia! Where's Reuben? You haven't let go of his lead have you? He's a bloodhound, seriously!' It was now about lunchtime and we hadn't found my egg yet, or Reuben, because Emelia dropped the lead! 'Reuben, here boy! Yes! He's just there. Oh dear, he's got something in his mouth which is bleeding. Drop!' I yelled and he did. We ran over to him and found... a dragon!

Evelyn Twigg (9)
Bowness-on-Solway Primary School, Wigton

Untitled

Carrie laid in bed, waiting for the clock to strike twelve. She watched it tick-tock round. Finally a cacophony of pings, dings and whooshes sent Carrie jumping out of bed, rushing into the wardrobe and coming out a superhero. She flung up the window and threw herself out. There was no problem for Carrie, she flew to the moon! Carrie went for an unusual night stroll along the craters of the moon. Suddenly, she fell down a crater. 'Argh!' She landed. 'Wow!' Carrie looked around this magical land. Just then she spotted an alien. 'Argh!'
'Blurp!'
She was gone!

Annabelle Wills (10)
Bowness-on-Solway Primary School, Wigton

Canine World

One glorious morning, the dogs in Canine World knew something was wrong. The dog handlers were cruel, and they seemed to be talking weird. One dog called Kipper squeezed through a hole. He thought they must be robots! Kipper got all of the dogs together and they had a talk. They said that he should go in and bite the cables. But smart dog Rover decided not to. So he cut the wires and the robots were dead. There were no robots again. Kipper was a hero.

James Paisley
Bowness-on-Solway Primary School, Wigton

Attack Of The Peas

During the night Zombpeas were munching on peas until... CJ the carrot came with the sweetcorn to get rid of the peas. The peas captured the village. CJ was with a zombtato who ate peas. Lots of peas were turning rotten, lots of peas were in Joe's belly, Joe being the zombtato. He was quite full, he went away. CJ was hiding until... *aaahhh!* CJ sprinted to the sound and Joe was getting bigger and bigger until he exploded into mashed zombtato!

Jack Sadler (10)
Bowness-on-Solway Primary School, Wigton

Dead Island Blood Sea

'Ugh! Aaahh!' John Morgan, Sam B, Xian, Purna, Logan and Hank were running as fast as they could away from a horde of blood-soaked zombies.
'Phew!' They just made it.
'Get the guns!' They blasted the door open.
'Die you ugly creatures!' *Bang! Bang!* In a few bullets – all the zombies had holes in them. They made it, they were at the safe zone, they could see the bridge. They ran until they saw the biggest horde of zombies they'd ever seen. They brought out the death machine and mauled them all, then they finally got to the safe zone.

Joe Irving (11)
Bowness-on-Solway Primary School, Wigton

I'm A Stone!

I woke up just when my alarm clock was going to ring. I heard
something clatter in my wardrobe. I opened the door and saw
a fairy amongst my clothes. My mum came in my room looking
tired. She asked me what I was doing and I replied, 'I'm looking for
something to wear today.'
'OK,' said Mum, 'but don't wake your father.'
I looked back in as I saw the fairy shivering with fear. I calmed her
down and then she turned me into a stone. So I stayed a stone for
the rest of my life.

Lana Twigg (8)
Bowness-on-Solway Primary School, Wigton

A Very Strange Day!

Sunshine started the day, it poured through the windows and filled the house with joy, Nova and Milly woke to their little brother Luke yelling like he did every morning. It was very annoying. This morning he was yelling extra loud so Nova got out of bed and shoved a sock in Luke's mouth, and Nova found it quite amusing. After the morning of yelling they had a lovely breakfast. As they all started to watch TV, something strange happened, they simply travelled back in time to the Jurassic period, and not just that, they turned into cave people!

Ellie Sheather (9)
Bowness-on-Solway Primary School, Wigton

Scorpion

There was a scorpion that was made out of lava, it could time travel. It transported to Snuse, past the galaxy, to its planet called Scorpion Dome. The lava scorpion had his throne there, and he planned to take over the world, but Jack, Ben and their army, planned to attack the scorpion king. But the scorpions transported to Earth to attack the humans! Thankfully, the humans had something that the scorpions didn't have... bazookas – *boom!* The scorpions retreated, screaming very loudly.

Kane Whitehead (9)
Bowness-on-Solway Primary School, Wigton

Candy Day

Today, on Planet Rainbowchock, it is Candy Day, it's the best day of the year. My name is Zig Teler. When you're me, Candy Day is the worst day of the year. I get teased and zappers say, 'You have a big head.' So I'm going to be a zapper, see how they like it.
Here comes one. 'Look here's big head!'
'Not as big as yours!'
There, now I've taught them a lesson. They'll never be mean again!

Kirsty Castles (9)
Bowness-on-Solway Primary School, Wigton

Bob The Dog

Bob the dog was only a puppy. One day he went to the zoo and he saw monkeys, but then he got lost. He was in with the snakes but he got out. Then he was in with the fish. Finally he found his way out and he went to the café. He was eating cake and it looked nice because it was chocolate cake!

Jonathan Wills (8)
Bowness-on-Solway Primary School, Wigton

Emily And Her Escape From An Old Man!

Once upon a time there lived a cute girl called Emily who lived with her bossy big brother Matthew. 'Please can we put the paddling pool and the slide out?' asked Emily.
'OK,' replied Matthew.
After they put their suits on they went down the slide and Emily fell down a big hole. 'Emily!' screamed Matthew. Matthew decided to go after her. After that Emily and Matthew found themselves in a lake, so they swam to the side. Then an old man grabbed Emily! Emily managed to escape after an hour and went to get Matthew from the lake.

Keira Louise Walker (9)
Cambridge Primary School, Barrow-In-Furness

Untitled

Once upon a time there was an extraordinary boy called Matt who was a minuscule Lego Man. Matt found out that not all monsters are bad. This boy called David wanted to kill the monsters, but Matt was going to do something about it. He said, 'Stop it or something is going to happen.' So he went to war and he pulled a remote out which changed the setting to a battlefield. 'We have war!' Matt had a choice to kill David, but he didn't want to. 'All I want is for you to be nice.'

Alan Falloon (8)
Cambridge Primary School, Barrow-In-Furness

Keira And The Evil Witch!

Once upon a time, there lived a girl called Keira. She lived in a huge castle with her two brothers Jake and Logan. One sunny day Keira and her brothers went to the beach. When they got there the witch Mrs Chalker shouted, 'Get off my beach!'
But they shouted, 'It is not your beach!'
Suddenly a police car arrived from behind them and took the witch away. After the witch got taken away, they all started to sunbathe until it was time for tea. After that they all celebrated the evil witch's arrest.

Imogen Ashton (8)
Cambridge Primary School, Barrow-In-Furness

The Powerful Gorilla

Once there was a gorilla who won all competitions, he was the most scariest and powerful gorilla anyone had ever seen. But one day he noticed that he was growing weak, so he went to Grandpa Ape who was 58 years old. He could help Lambo but he said Lambo had to go to the volcano! Lambo travelled miles through forests, oceans, deserts and mountains, but where was the volcano? Lambo started to chuckle, he was facing the wrong way. He marched up the volcano, it started to shake and exploded with flames. Nobody's seen him since that day!

Breeanna Corkill (8)
Cambridge Primary School, Barrow-In-Furness

The Fight Of A Winner

'Bye,' shouted Stella when Juliet and Bloom left Alfea, the fairy school, so they could see Leona the dolphin. When they got to the flowing crystal sea, Leona was singing. 'Leona,' shouted Juliet and Bloom. 'Where are you?'

'I'm here,' said Leona.

'Well I wanted to say...'

'Stop! I have a bad feeling.'

'Surprise!' said the ice witch.

'Well looky what we have here, it's Trix. Why are you here?'

'To fight!'

At that moment, Bloom and Juliet transformed, and started fighting Trix. Because of how powerful Juliet and Bloom were, they were triumphant. Then Trix disappeared like magic!

Leanne Southward (8)
Cambridge Primary School, Barrow-In-Furness

Attack Of The Authority

Once, at a TLC match, a lunatic called Dean sat and watched. His friend fought Bray Wyatt, his friend, won.

One day Dean met his friends John Cena, Roman Reigns and Big Show. They discovered a group named 'The Authority'. They had, Auntie Rollins, Uncle Kane and Granny H. When they found each other, H asked to team, but they didn't want to. So Rollins tried to attack the Authority but H pulled him back. Then they all attacked each other, the Authority had an advantage, then suddenly Dean jumped in. He was triumphant and saved them all!

Jake Holmes (9)
Cambridge Primary School, Barrow-In-Furness

Once Upon A Time

Many years ago, there was a baby and a queen and a king, they lived in a beautiful castle. They decided to move far away, so they could be rich. They moved to another country and they had a party in the castle. They invited three fairy godmothers, one made the baby able to fly, one gave her snow powers, and one gave her love. Years later, the princess was dancing at a ball, she met a prince who asked her for a dance. She said yes! They kissed and after that day they married and lived happily ever after.

Elise Olga Charnley (8)
Cambridge Primary School, Barrow-In-Furness

The Wicked Witch!

One day there was a wicked witch that wanted to destroy the world. But there were guards guarding it. So she couldn't take control. Then a man went out to get some wood, but suddenly he stepped into a trap! The wicked witch came and she took him to the cellar, she wanted to know where the magical pearl was, but he didn't know.

Three days later someone came to rescue him. He escaped and found the magical pearl. Then he threw it off the world, and the evil wicked witch died. He lived happily ever after.

Kate Hardman (9)
Cambridge Primary School, Barrow-In-Furness

The Scary Sea Monster

Once upon a time dolphins were playing in the blue water. Suddenly a hungry sea monster swam near. Suddenly the sea monster took the dolphins' food. The dolphins were angry but also scared. Inger the dolphin tried to be brave, and chased the red monster. The sea monster roared and caught him in his large jaws. Inger was taken away and the other dolphins were sad. Joey and Clown chased the sea monster into a dark cave, there was a fierce fight between the dolphins and the sea monster.The dolphins killed the sea monster. Hooray!

Richard Bown (8)
Cambridge Primary School, Barrow-In-Furness

Incredible Apes' Life

There was a dark, gloomy cave, it was no ordinary cave because a lot of apes lived there. It was a long cave where workers worked much harder than humans. Apes bonded with robots that lived nearby.

Every year the president's special force would try and capture them, but the apes dug a hole and hid there until they were gone. Then they would go back to work. Only fifteen apes had been taken and put down.

But one year later they caught a man dressed up as a robot. They locked him in prison, where he died a gruesome death.

Logan Garner (8)
Cambridge Primary School, Barrow-In-Furness

The Cheetah Killed The Wolf

Once upon a time there lived a cheetah family and they went to find some meat, so they could eat it. They had to kill the prey first. Speedy the mother cheetah was with her two cubs and their names were Zooma and Zap. Speedy could hear something so she went to find out what she could hear. Speedy saw lots of moose, and they killed the biggest moose, and they all had tea. Then they all fell asleep. After they fell asleep, the wolf came and took some of the meat to eat. The cheetah killed the wolf.

Stephanie Marie Carter (9)
Cambridge Primary School, Barrow-In-Furness

Untitled

Once upon a time there was a rhino called Walter. The atmosphere was the most deadly in the world. Walter was fierce and scary with thick skin. He was as mean as my sister. The animals were tired of Walter being mean, and hurting them, so one day they came up with a cunning plan, the plan was to kidnap Walter's little sister...

Kingsley Craig (9)
Cambridge Primary School, Barrow-In-Furness

Untitled

Once upon a time there was a girl called Pearl and she was in a forest alone. She was walking to the shops and there were two types of monsters. They were really scary, and they had a bad and grumpy mood. Then she noticed that there was a magical spell on them, that made them go to sleep. When they fell asleep she went back home to get some monster food because the monsters were hungry. She gave the monsters the food and they decided to be her friends. They would play with each other every week.

Brooke Alderson (8)
Cambridge Primary School, Barrow-In-Furness

The Poor Christmas Tree

There was once a Christmas tree, he was a poor Christmas tree, his friends got sold, he was alone in the blackness. To start with he was very scared. Outside he heard a car engine, he begged for the car to turn left. The car owners felt so sorry for the lonely Christmas tree, so they took him. He was very excited! After a while they stopped, the Christmas tree was very happy. The owners of the car took the Christmas tree inside, so they could decorate him with baubles and tinsel. It was tickly, he laughed very loudly.

Kacey Procter (8)
Grange CE Primary School, Grange-Over-Sands

The 40 Ill Elves

Once upon a time there were 40 elves. In December all the elves got the flu. Santa had to wrap the presents, he thought that he would get all of them done, but he didn't. So he tweeted everyone in 96 languages to say, 'I am changing Christmas Day to 30th December and Boxing Day to the 31st of December.'
When the wrapping was finished, they set off on the new Christmas Day. Everyone was happy, apart from someone because he never got any presents because Santa forgot!

Alice Walmsley (7)
Grange CE Primary School, Grange-Over-Sands

Beast Quest – Koron
The Vanished Viper

Tom looked at the map of the bark, he got it when he defeated Heckon. He scanned it. 'Our next beast should be in the vanished woodland,' he said to Elena. They galloped over to the woodland. 'Well this is it,' said Tom, staring at it.
Tom and Elena leapt off Storm and Blizzard. They ran in. 'Whoa!' Tom shouted. He had tripped over a tomb lever, in seconds a viper crashed out, he shot venom, Tom scanned it. 'Aha! Its weak spot!' Tom jumped, hit it with his sword – *boom,* it exploded. They ran out. 'Hooray!' they shouted.

Ross Best (8)
Grange CE Primary School, Grange-Over-Sands

The Gingerbread Secret

A long time ago, there was a gingerbread man who ran away from the bakery. He was the smartest gingerbread man in the bakery. Anyone could see him because he kept running into the kitchen. One night, in winter, he got fed up so he ran into the woods. He accidentally ran into the deepest part of the woods. He was scared, so he ran into a green sparkly tree with a door. He bumped into the door. As he got up he looked around. He thought it was a perfect place to live, so started to dance – *Snap!*

Diya Elizabeth Biju Chempananikel (8)
Grange CE Primary School, Grange-Over-Sands

The Snow Fairy

One snowy night there was a snow fairy, her name was Katie. She lived on a snowy mountain. She had a friend, she was called Ella, she lived on the same mountain.

One night there was a *bump clump!* It was Santa! 'Ho! Ho! Ho!' But they didn't see him.

That morning they woke up. 'Let's make a snow fairy,' said Ella. The next morning all the snow melted, under the tree there were loads of presents! They unwrapped all the presents, they both got some new wings, they were sparkly gold.

Erin Hathorn (7)
Grange CE Primary School, Grange-Over-Sands

The Ice Dragon

Sassi the ice dragon was being played with by a boy named Leo.
They were having so much fun until it was bedtime for Leo. So Leo
said, 'See you tomorrow.' Little did Leo know that the dragon was
alive.
Suddenly the dragon heard the rumbling of its enemies, he began
to run then fly. Then he looked down and started to fly up, it was
easy for him to fly. Finally he made a trap and the enemies got
trapped in a rubber cage. Yay!

Leo Michael Macdonald (7)
Grange CE Primary School, Grange-Over-Sands

The Ice Beast

Luke fell to the ground, he'd just defeated the latest beast. There was only one more beast to defeat, but he'd heard that it was the hardest! He was walking across the snow and ice until he saw something moving slowly, covered in ice! It was shuddering in a frightful way. Its eyes were glowing red with anger at Luke. He raised his sword, ready to swing at the beast. The beast shot out a big ice ball. Luke sliced it with fire power and sent a burning ice bomb back, the beast died. He'd saved the world!

William Morrell (7)
Grange CE Primary School, Grange-Over-Sands

Lego Christmas

There was a Lego figure called Max, he was a little boy and he loved Christmas. On one Christmas Eve he decided that he would stay up and see Santa. He waited and waited... Hours passed that seemed like days! 'I'm bored!' said Max to himself. 'How long will this take?'

Suddenly he heard a *clunk*, he went downstairs to see what it was... Santa! His dream had come true. Max was thrilled, he did not know what to say. Then he saw a red shiny sleigh with eight reindeer!

Isaac Johnston (7)
Grange CE Primary School, Grange-Over-Sands

The Snow Dog And The Snowman

There was once a snowman and a snow dog, they went
everywhere together, but one day the snowman went missing.
Then the snow dog was all alone, so the snow dog went to find
him. He went to the woods but he wasn't there. He said to himself,
'I miss you.'
Suddenly, there he was walking towards the woods. They ran
towards each other and they had a big hug. Then they went back to
their field.

Jayden Latham Saunders (7)
Grange CE Primary School, Grange-Over-Sands

Bee Attack

One day at the beehive there was a discussion that there would be a fight between the bees and the people. The bees were determined to win the battle.
The day came and the bees would strike at 11 o'clock. They were just getting ready when the people opened the beehive and stared at them, and then tried to take the honey. Then the bees struck back by stinging them. The people ran away. Some returned. They had to replan their fight.
The next day the bees were ready, they had the fight and the bees won!

Samuel Jackson (8)
Grange CE Primary School, Grange-Over-Sands

The Christmas Present

Santa was working with the elves. On Christmas Eve Santa went to everyone. A little boy opened his present, it was a robot. He played with it until bedtime.

The next morning he woke up, his robot was dancing! He could hear people shouting outside, so he took his robot outside. The robot chucked a snowball at the boy's friends. They chucked snowballs at the robot. It turned into a snowball fight! The boy had a great time and his robot did too.

Dan Phillips (8)
Grange CE Primary School, Grange-Over-Sands

The Snowman

A boy was excited. 'Christmas!' It was snowing so he went outside, he built a snowman. There was something he didn't know... the snowman was magical. His dad called him in to go to bed. At midnight he woke up because he saw a flash, he went downstairs and there it was again! So he went into the garden. The snowman raised his hat, he ran with the boy, they started to fly. They saw a Christmas tree up ahead, he met Santa. He gave the boy a present. Santa gave them a ride home. 'Ho! Ho! Ho!'

Alfie Boydell (7)
Grange CE Primary School, Grange-Over-Sands

The Day I Was Not At Home

A glimmer of light shone through a gap between the curtains. 'Hang on a minute, where am I? Those aren't my curtains?'
I noticed that I was in a tree, someone was at the door, it was a small goblin. 'Why are you making such a racket?' said the goblin.
'Where am I?'
'You're in the world of Lego.'
'You mean this is made out of Lego?'
'Yes, all of it is!' Well I wanted to get home so we made a time machine. 'You can go back now!'
'Finally! Yippee!'

Thomas Mallinson (7)
Grange CE Primary School, Grange-Over-Sands

The Snail And The Dog

Once upon a time there was a brown dog, he thought he was the best! A snail wandered past and he was upset. The dog made the snail have a race to prove the dog was best, the snail thought otherwise. 'Ready, steady go!' the dog shouted. They were off! Well, the dog was. The dog ran and ran until he got tired, the dog sat down by a tree and fell asleep! Soon the snail caught up and the snail went on and won the race. Eventually, the dog woke up, and the dog realised he hadn't won!

Matthew Barker (10)
Grange CE Primary School, Grange-Over-Sands

Gamer

Charlie loved playing Minecraft. One day Charlie was playing Minecraft. Suddenly he got sucked into the game! He screamed like a girl, but he enjoyed it after a while. He made friends with Steve and his pet dog. Then he got out of Minecraft, and he went into Skylander. It was amazing!
After a few hours Charlie got out. He went to the library with his mum. Charlie went on the computer there. He went into Mario Kart and Charlie won all of the races.

Cameron Barnsley (8)
Grange CE Primary School, Grange-Over-Sands

Spot's Missing Bones

'Spot, it's munching time!' his mum called.
Spot sprinted to his dog bowl... There was not even a scrap left!
'Awooo! Where's my juicy bones, Mum?'
She ran as fast as she could. 'Darlin' what's wrong?' Spot
explained what was wrong. 'Oh no... it was that pesky rat!'
They set off on the quest to find Spot's bones. 'Look... rat poo. It's
evidence.'
They followed the path ahead. Rat was in his hole. 'There he is,
give me my bones back... !'
'OK.'

Leila Higgins (8)
Grange CE Primary School, Grange-Over-Sands

Foxy Saves The Day!

Barry, Clifford, Isaac and Max, four chubby robins, all sat in a big bramble bush. The snow was falling, the wind was blowing, down below Foxy was hungry for a meal.

Brian the jolly farmer was working in a nearby field. He stopped to rest and saw the bramble bush. Brian moved closer to the bush where the robins chatted away. The bush was just what Brian needed for his Christmas decorations. He began to chop, Foxy leapt frightening Brian who ran. *Tea...* thought Foxy and chased Brian.

'Hooray,' chirped the robins. 'Foxy has saved the day, thank you!'

Samuel Herrema (9)
Grange CE Primary School, Grange-Over-Sands

Big Bad Hedgehog

One winter day, in the snow, Big Bad Hedgehog was on his way to the shops. He knew he had to cross the road. This was a problem. He could not see the cars because of the snow. This was going to be hard, he thought for a moment and remembered that time his dad had died. He was crossing the road. What if that happened to Big Bad Hedgehog? So he puffed, huffed, took a deep breath, and looked side to side... he was lucky. Finally he got to the shops, he spent his money, and lived happily ever after.

Amelie Taylor (8)
Grange CE Primary School, Grange-Over-Sands

The Christmas Surprise

One Christmas Eve, there was a little boy who loved Christmas, but his big sister didn't believe in Santa. When it was bedtime, he was so excited.

In the morning the boy ran downstairs but his smile turned upside down when he saw no presents! Suddenly he saw someone behind him. It was Santa! His sister couldn't believe it, nobody could! But the little boy knew he was real.

'You have been a good little boy,' said Santa, giving him his presents. 'Have a merry Christmas. Bye-bye.'

Jayden James Reading (9)
Grange CE Primary School, Grange-Over-Sands

The Boy Who Might Have Learnt His Lesson

There was once a menace. It was edging near Christmas, and his mum was sure he was on the naughty list. Preston, who was the horrible menace, had a big wish list this year.
It was Christmas Eve and most people would be eager to open their calendars, but Preston had eaten all the chocolates. Preston's mum gave him £10 to spend on Christmas presents for relatives. Guess what, he spent it all on menacing jokes all for himself.
On Christmas Day he woke up with a grin on his face, not knowing the surprise that awaited him... !

Kira McLaughlin (9)
Grange CE Primary School, Grange-Over-Sands

The Mythical Magic Tennis Ball

One day a boy named Jack took a trip to the museum. He stumbled around looking at all the boring things, but one thing caught his eye, it was a sort of ball, a tennis ball, with glowing colours. It said in bold: *Do Not Touch!* but it was too tempting. He took one touch, he saw a white flash, *bang!* He was in a world of sweets! As he looked around he saw a big yellow gummy bear, it started chasing him! Jack screamed as the gummy bear tumbled over him... A white flash, and he was back!

Evie Dobson (10)
Grange CE Primary School, Grange-Over-Sands

Christmas Pudding Day

'Christmas Pudding Day!' Bob said. But the bad thing was inspectors were there.
'Right let's get baking, what do you need to make? Yes, Christmas pudding,' Bob's teacher said. But it was a disaster! Some of the Christmas pudding got stuck to the ceiling, it was smelly and burnt. The inspector came in. The Christmas pudding went on the inspector. The inspector ran away, but they made another one to calm him down. The inspector came back, ate the Christmas pudding and sang 'Jingle Bells'. Thay all had such fun together. They got full marks. Yay!

Joe Taylor (10)
Grange CE Primary School, Grange-Over-Sands

The Tale Of A Squirrel And Santa

One day a squirrel woke up out of hibernation because a random polar bear had been sniffing around his acorns. The squirrel was freezing and he needed somewhere to keep warm. Luckily he spotted a cave, so he rushed inside. The only problem was it wasn't a cave, it was a massive workshop. Elves were crafting magnificent toys and gifts so the squirrel decided to have a look around. Suddenly, he bumped into Santa! He directed the squirrel to a workshop and told him to make over 300 toys. It sure was going to be a long night...

Herbie Harrison (10)
Grange CE Primary School, Grange-Over-Sands

Saving The Santas

Once upon a time, a long time ago, there were a few Santas all around the world, but they kept disappearing. One day Santa, the only one left, called a meeting with all the magical creatures. He shouted, 'I've had enough of this, we need to stop this!' So everyone around the world tried.
One day an elf said he saw the chief elf putting traps everywhere. The elf was banished and the Santas returned.
That week everybody was celebrating until somebody shouted, 'Where's the Christmas tree?'
Oh no who took it? Did the chief elf take it...?

Grace Davis (9)
Grange CE Primary School, Grange-Over-Sands

The Underwater Alien

Charlie wanted a Christmas tree. But he was an alien who lived underwater. He really wanted one, so in the middle of the night he set off. But he couldn't exactly ask anyone for a tree, so he climbed the highest hill to the tree farm. He'd arrived. He looked at all the trees, which one should he choose? He picked out a fairly big sized tree, and put it through the netting then left a few pounds, and he was gone!

Mia Best (10)
Grange CE Primary School, Grange-Over-Sands

Chicken Vs Snowman

A chicken sat in his tree house. Suddenly, it began to shake. A lump of snow leapt through the window. The snowman, who'd just formed, asked the chicken whether they could be friends. The yellow-feathered bundle agreed. Their friendship was strong, but the snowman desperately wanted the tree house.
One day, when they were sitting in the tree house, the envious plotter squirted a lump of snow right at his friend! Feathers flew and snow bounced as the battle raged. Eventually the chicken managed to push the snowman out the window. He'd triumphed! He eyed the snowman as he melted.

Ross (10)
Grange CE Primary School, Grange-Over-Sands

The Little White Mouse

The great, grey wolf tried to deliver a present to little white mouse. The bears wanted to save her, so they hit the wolf on the head, so they could save little white mouse. After that little white mouse had a picnic with the bears. When the wolf turned up the bears pulled some rope and a cage fell down on the wolf. The wolf said, 'I've only got a present for little white mouse.' The bears took the cage off because they realised that the wolf wasn't bad after all. 'Come to the picnic with us,' said the bears.

Daisy McLaughlin (6)
Grange CE Primary School, Grange-Over-Sands

The Dress Disaster

Once upon a time, there was a beautiful princess called Emily. She was so happy because she had a pretty blue dress.
One day, when Princess Emily was running, the shiny gold beads fell off her dress. She was very sad. Just then Libby came over to Emily and said, 'What's happened?'
Princess Emily told Libby that she wanted the shiny beads back on her dress, so Libby said, 'Don't worry, I will help you to find the beads, and put them back on your dress.'
'Oh thank you, you are a super friend,' and off they went.

Emily Williams (7)
Grange CE Primary School, Grange-Over-Sands

Christmas Is A Disaster

There was a husky dog and a pale brown reindeer. On Christmas Eve Reindeer took Dog to the North Pole. They were greeted by a freezing penguin wearing a hat and gloves, who took them to Santa's workshop. As they entered, Dog smelt a tasty treat. He ran and accidentally crashed into the conveyor belt. Santa's workshop ground to a halt! Dog, Reindeer, Santa and his elves had to make all the presents by hand. Dog found his treat, but it took forever to make all the toys by hand. The presents weren't ready until the first of January!

Sean Kerr (6)
Grange CE Primary School, Grange-Over-Sands

Winter Land

There was a mouse who had dark red eyes and it was grey with a long tail and the mouse was called Bob. A nice elephant was called Stanley, and his tusks were shiny and he had a very long tail and scruffy nails. Stanley got very angry every time he saw an insect. He saw an ant. The ant was scared, so the mouse calmed him down. They became friends and took the ant home and had tea there and they got cold, then they put the fire on. It started snowing, and the ant and mouse were happy.

Caleb Higgins (6)
Grange CE Primary School, Grange-Over-Sands

Santa Napped

One cold Christmas Day, a little girl called Katey went downstairs to find the most horrifying thing ever, there were no presents, and Rudolph was in her house eating figgy pudding! Santa must have been Santa napped! She wandered outside, all she found was Santa's very cold fragile hat. There was a tunnel, she followed it then there was Santa, upside down in the snow, with a present next to him. She opened it. Just what she wanted, a book called 'The Night Before Christmas'. She rescued Santa, gave him a warm cup of milk and read her book.

Skye Scholey (9)
Grange CE Primary School, Grange-Over-Sands

Evil Adventure

Once there was a panda who loved the outside, but he was never allowed outside until he was old enough. When he was old enough he went out to explore. He climbed out of the window and over the fence to explore. He found a forest so he went into the forest and found a monkey. They became friends and carried on. The monkey was swinging above the panda. But the panda couldn't climb trees, so he was just walking on the hard, bumpy ground. The panda tripped over two black boots, put them on, flew up and never came back!

Alex Otway (9)
Grange CE Primary School, Grange-Over-Sands

Mr Bogam At Work

Mr Bogam was evil! He'd always wanted to spoil Christmas, he hated seeing people happy. There was 13 days till Christmas and Bogam had made an army of electronic snowmen to kidnap Santa. Mr Bogam got his supercharged sleigh and went to the North Pole with his army of robot snowmen. When he got there he knocked on the door. Santa came out and he was stuffed into a sack. They flew for hours until *bang!* The sack ripped open on the roof. Santa escaped, Christmas was saved. Bogam didn't notice... 'I've spoilt Christmas!' he laughed to himself.

Thomas Ashley (9)
Grange CE Primary School, Grange-Over-Sands

The Mystical Sea

The small, white, fluffy dog went to the sea. He dipped his paws in just to test the temperature. It was a brilliant temperature. He went in, his paws started to disappear and turned into a fish tail, then his body turned into a slimy green fish body, then he turned into a full fish! So he went for a swim all around the sea. He got caught in seaweed and got dragged to a cave. Just then a boat dropped a gas tank into the water, and killed all of the fish, but him...

Gemma Lacey (9)
Grange CE Primary School, Grange-Over-Sands

Naughty Or Nice?

Billy, who was very grumpy, loved Christmas because of all the presents. He had no idea that he was on the naughty list. Billy didn't believe in Santa, he thought it was made up.
Suddenly his mum walked in the door with a letter from Santa. She dropped it on his bed. Billy walked over and read the letter. It said that he was on the naughty list. Billy didn't care, so he chucked it in the bin. At night the snow crashed against the ground, the storm whirled against his window. Suddenly, he heard a *crash!* He woke up... !

Tom Agliolo (9)
Grange CE Primary School, Grange-Over-Sands

Sappa And Dodo

There were two teddies called Sappa and Dodo. They liked going on crazy, weird adventures. 'I think we are going into space today,' said Sappa. They went behind a dark and gloomy bookcase. Dodo pressed the red spiky button and took a deep breath. At once they were zooming through the sky like rockets. On the way there, Sappa went out of control and bumped his backside on the white moon. So they had a quick bounce around because they had teddy tennis to get changed for. Unfortunately they drove too fast, and crashed into Mars with a *bam!*

Idris Illingworth (7)
Grange CE Primary School, Grange-Over-Sands

Story About Animals

There were loads of animals. The animals were trying to find some tea. But they couldn't find any because all the other animals had eaten it. So the animals didn't have any. The animals were so hungry and sad so they went back home without any tasty tea. They were so sad and hungry all day, but then a surprise came. It was some tea. Then they were so happy that they did a little dance to celebrate, and then they ate and drank very quickly. Then they went back to sleep, and they were so tired after their day.

Patrycja Polec (6)
Grange CE Primary School, Grange-Over-Sands

The Super Snowman And The Aliens

A super snowman saved the world from an alien invasion. The aliens were capturing the babies but Super Snowman killed the aliens with a karate kick and a snow gun, but one of the masters didn't die, so he called for more aliens to fight.
Then a reindeer came shooting from the sky and really helped Super Snowman, and Super Snowman called him Snuggles.
So they fought together. Snuggles killed the master and Super Snowman was so happy that he gave Snuggles two carrots for killing the master of the aliens. They were really happy afterwards.

Vincent Lacey (6)
Grange CE Primary School, Grange-Over-Sands

Robert The Robot

Robert the rusty red robot wanted to see the moon close up so he tried to jump up and up but he couldn't reach, so he went to find a small spaceship. He then found a spaceship and went inside and it was time to count down... 5, 4, 3, 2, 1... blast-off! As he floated into the deep, dark, starry space, he felt excited because he could finally see the bumpy, bright, white moon. Robert had a rough landing on the moon, but he jumped out of the spaceship and bounced around on the moon!

Roshana Joy Higginson (6)
Grange CE Primary School, Grange-Over-Sands

A Dangerous Snowflake

It was Christmas, Izzy was making a snowflake out of white paper.
She made a dangerous snowflake. It was alive! When it touched
you it would freeze you into a statue. She left her bedroom window
open. Suddenly a gust of wind blew through her bedroom, and it
began to float out of the window.
Seren, Heather and Idris were making a snowman in their back
garden. The dangerous snowflake touched the children on their
shoulders, the children froze. Izzy was shocked. Izzy decided to
capture the snowflake and threw it into the recycling bin.

Paige McLaughlin (6)
Grange CE Primary School, Grange-Over-Sands

The Evil Bird

There was a little bird, who was evil. The bird wanted to destroy everything. The bird used its powers to help it destroy the city, but the people of the city made a snowman to defeat the evil bird. Quickly, the snowman suggested fighting in the burning hot sun. It was harder for the evil bird but the snowman was secretly a robot. It was easier for the snowman because he was a robot. The evil bird got burnt and had to fly away.

Heather Lowes (7)
Grange CE Primary School, Grange-Over-Sands

Gangsta Santa

One snowy morning an elf came trotting through Santa's grotto, getting presents ready. He was one happy elf. But just then he saw a shadow running across the road. The shadow turned around. 'Ahhh! Guess what? It was Santa! Santa's a gangsta!' Every elf was looking at Santa, they looked more confused, then Santa was tickling a feather up his nose!
Santa walked through the door. He said, 'I am not a gangsta!'
'Then why are you dressed in that costume?'
'I was only going to the shop to buy some bread!'

Mary Phoebe Dobson (8)
Grange CE Primary School, Grange-Over-Sands

The Missing Pug

One dark night, Dave, Lisa and Doug went camping. The next
morning they went for a walk. Suddenly... Doug went missing... !
Dave and Lisa knew he was somewhere in the woods.
'Doug, Doug, come on we have your toy. We should have kept an
eye on him,' Dave said.
Lisa and Dave decided to look for Doug, but they couldn't see a
thing as it was getting dark. They had to go back to the tent.
When they got back all they could hear was *ruff, ruff, ruff!* It was
Doug! The clever dog had found the tent.
'Well done!'

Sophia Elle Maher (8)
Grange CE Primary School, Grange-Over-Sands

The Pug Dog

One dark night, Doug needed the loo so he went to wake the owners up. He couldn't wake them up, he wasn't loud enough, he thought he should bark louder at the owners. The owners woke up. 'Let's go downstairs,' said Karl. Doug ran and ran. They opened the door. Doug went out, went to the loo then came inside and went to bed.

The next morning Doug woke up and Amy and Karl woke up. 'Walkies!' Amy said. 'Go and get your lead.' He went into the kitchen and got it. 'Let's go Doug!' He ran zooming off.

Jayden Lewis Buchan (9)
Grange CE Primary School, Grange-Over-Sands

Millie Moo's Mouse Dilemma

Millie Moo woke on another glorious day. She suddenly realised the pesky mouse had stolen her favourite toy... again! She knew she needed to trap the mouse in a mousetrap. She set them all around the house, and then she heard a *bang!* It was the sound of a trap. She scampered to find the trap. When she got there she found the mouse! 'I will let you go if you give me my toys back.'
'OK,' said the mouse. 'Here, now let me go.'
'Noo!' Millie gobbled up the mouse!

Ryelainn Scholey (8)
Grange CE Primary School, Grange-Over-Sands

Zombie Apocalypse

One dark night, in a graveyard, a person called Steve was walking around when all of a sudden something caught his eye! A whole army of people were walking slowly to him then he heard something. He said, 'Argh, run, it's the zombie apocalypse!' Then Steve turned around, there were some more. He quickly ran to his car, but Steve forgot his way to the city to warn people of the zombie apocalypse. Then Steve helped fight the zombies and wanted to find out who unleashed them.

Jack Williams (8)
Grange CE Primary School, Grange-Over-Sands

The Chick

Once upon a time, there was a chick, a very small chick that couldn't fly. All her brothers and sisters were flying around her. She was very annoyed, angry and gloomy. She was so tempted to do this awesome and amazing thing. So she went up to a steep cliff and she jumped! Safely and carefully she flew, she was amazed by this and now she knew how to fly, she did a backflip, but she fell. Amazingly she was safe, floating with her wings in the chilly, night air. So she flew home, satisfied.

Hilton Yener Etisoy (8)
St Herbert's CE Primary & Nursery School, Keswick

The Rich Man

Once upon a time there was a rich man, who had a bingo game, he played it all night and he lost all his money. He was very tearful and gloomy thinking about his money. If he hadn't lost all his money he would have been the King of England, however the man who won all the glittering money was now the King of England. He must be very pleased and jolly.

The poor man remembered that he had a Lotto ticket and he checked the lottery and he won all his precious money back.

Thomas Price
St Herbert's CE Primary & Nursery School, Keswick

The King And The Queen

Once upon a time there was a queen and a king. On a cosy Friday morning in November the queen lost her crown. There was a sparkling, golden diamond door. She went through it into the forest. It was a very scorching day. She looked for her crown in the forest. A squirrel had put it up a silver birch tree. She found a man with a chainsaw. He cut the tree down and she got her crown back. She took it back and the door appeared. The king never knew it was missing.

Oliver Pepper
St Herbert's CE Primary & Nursery School, Keswick

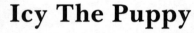

Icy The Puppy

Once upon a time there was a beautiful puppy called Icy. She was always looking for mischievous things to do. It was finally Christmas Eve and all the house was fast asleep... until a gargantuan *bang!* came from the chimney. Icy dashed through to the gloomy kitchen, but no one was there, so gratefully, she strolled back to her basket. Later, Icy got up and crept into the living room and pounced onto an enormous man! He said, 'Would you like to come and live at the North Pole?'
'Of course,' Icy said, and they sprinted off into the peaceful night.

Ebony Sienna Heels (8)
St Herbert's CE Primary & Nursery School, Keswick

Rudolph's Adventure

It was Christmas Eve, Santa was getting ready. Oh no! Santa
tripped over a present and broke his leg! Santa said, 'Rudolph, you
must deliver the presents to the people this year.'
Rudolph agreed and went out into the cold night sky and started
delivering.
It was midnight and Rudolph was nowhere near done. He looked
at his magical collar that helped the reindeer deliver presents.
Rudolph thought now was the time to use it. All the presents went
to the right house.
It was almost morning, Rudolph was finally home. Santa rewarded
him with a massive, crunchy bright orange carrot.

Lauren Emily Garty (7)
St Herbert's CE Primary & Nursery School, Keswick

Christmas

Once upon a time there were three kids who woke up on Christmas Day. They went downstairs with their parents and opened up their colossal presents. Then they had their best dinner of the year – Christmas dinner! Their dad cooked the dinner. After that good dinner they had their pudding. Later they put the Christmas tree up and then started to decorate the tree, putting baubles and really nice pictures of angels and candy canes and a star right on the top of the Christmas tree. The tree looked wonderful when it was finished with all the lovely Christmas decorations.

Dylan Speight (8)
St Herbert's CE Primary & Nursery School, Keswick

Charlotte's Food Fight

There was once a girl called Charlotte and she loved to have parties! However she always caused trouble. Then one day, she had a party and she invited everyone in her class! Everyone said yes and when it was the day of the party everyone turned up and had a great boogie! Then... it was the food time! Time for Charlotte's special topping to it all. Suddenly, Charlotte shouted, 'Stop!'
Everyone stopped eating and said, 'What?'
Then Charlotte shouted back, 'Food fight!' and started throwing food at people, so they started throwing it back. It was a great day!

Charlotte Andrews (10)
St Margaret Mary Catholic Primary School, Carlisle

Santa's Elves

In a faraway land lived Santa and his elves. It was getting nearer to Christmas and Santa hadn't got all the Christmas presents ready. He thought he was in a great deal of trouble. Every year Santa had the presents ready early. Santa had only one thing left to save the amazing job he had been given, he would have to help the elves get the presents ready. This would help him lose a little bit of weight. Time flew by and it was Christmas Eve. Santa still had a lot of presents to wrap. Could he do it... ?

Emily Taylor (10)
St Margaret Mary Catholic Primary School, Carlisle

Olaf Saves The World

Once upon a time there was a magic snowman named Olaf, he was on a mission to save the world from exploding. He sailed the seven seas and came through a jungle with angry snakes, roaring lions, a dark frog jumping all over him. Did he survive? Oh yes, he survived evil monkeys trying to catch him! Suddenly an elephant came, *stomp, stomp*. He finally pushed his way out of the jungle. In the distance was an island, there were demons who were bombing his world! He swam and swam and swam and swam till he got there!

Ruby Perrett (8)
St Margaret Mary Catholic Primary School, Carlisle

Ruby The Halloween Bunny

Once upon a time there was a white fluffy rabbit called Ruby. Ruby was asleep when she was woken up by scary sounds. It was Halloween but she never knew what this was. Ruby went to see what was going on. She joined in and they played tig. Then they played hide-and-seek. Ruby hid behind a tree and she never got found for a very long time. Some scary monsters took Ruby trick or treating. They all knocked on doors and said, 'The sky is blue, the grass is green, have you anything for Halloween?'

Amelia Dixon (5)
St Margaret Mary Catholic Primary School, Carlisle

Olaf's Quest!

There once lived a snowman called Olaf who loved quests. Once he had saved the world from a big snow monster who was very strong. Suddenly a letter came through the door of his icy snow house. Olaf opened it, mysteriously it was a quest from the queen, it read: 'Dear Olaf, I have a very important quest for you today. I want you to sail over the Atlantic Ocean and try to find the Loch Ness monster. Good luck Olaf'. So Olaf set off over the ocean in search of the Loch Ness monster.

Ruby Grace Henry (9)
St Margaret Mary Catholic Primary School, Carlisle

Bell

Once upon a time there was a beautiful princess called Belle. She had a wicked stepsister called Matha and stepbrother called Edith and a wicked stepmother. Belle didn't get on with her new family. All of the family got an important letter from Prince James who was having a ball. Belle found some old clothes and her nice friends made her a dress but her stepsister ripped her dress up. She ran into the garden and was crying on the bench. Her fairy godmother came...
She went to the ball and found her true love!

Heather Christina Amot (9)
St Margaret Mary Catholic Primary School, Carlisle

The Tiger And The Snake

Once, in a small jungle, lived a courageous tiger who wanted to face a slow snake in a five hundred mile race. After time passed it was time for the big race. Nevertheless, the snake was thinking the tiger would sprint and get tired.

Eventually, the race began. The tiger roared, 'Eat my dust,' and he was gone in a flash.

After two hours the tiger was exhausted then fell asleep. After a while the snake overtook the beastly tiger, then surprisingly won the grand race. Now the snake was the fastest in the Amazon jungle!

Nadine Thomlinson (9)
St Margaret Mary Catholic Primary School, Carlisle

Ibe's Adventure

One day Ibe was sitting in his hill. 'Sigh, I'm so lonely. I want some friends.' So he packed some tins of beans and set off through the magical waterfall guarding his hill. 'Finally, I've reached the forest, I've heard it's filled with magical creatures.'
Meanwhile, in a field by a village, some other monsters were saying, 'I'm bored.'
'It's boring here, I am going to find a new place to live.'
At last Ibe reached the village. The bored monsters were named Dibe, Brid and Cibe. Soon Ibe was their friend, they packed up and went home with him.

Freya Ackley (9)
St Margaret Mary Catholic Primary School, Carlisle

Box Boy

One day, in a street called Charlie Road, a boy called Charlie found a pink box, he went home and got a pair of bolt cutters. He tried so hard to open it, his face went red. Then he threw it down the stairs. After that he tried to feed it some chocolate but it didn't eat it so he ate it instead! So he went outside to try to open it. An old man came and said, 'That's a brick you know.' Then he went home but still the boy tried to open it!

Shannon White (9)
St Margaret Mary Catholic Primary School, Carlisle

Joe The Racer

One day there was a boy called Joe, he was a pro racer. He entered loads of races and won them. Once there was a big race and he entered. He was confident he would win, but he found out that there was even more pro racers! He was ready though!
The day arrived, he was about to set off, 3, 2, 1... go! Joe set off, holding the pedal down as hard as he could. He barged into someone and right now he was first, then he skidded, he slid, turned, and then... won!

Joe Armstrong (10)
St Margaret Mary Catholic Primary School, Carlisle

A Man Who Woke Up On A Football Pitch

One day a man woke up from a deep sleep, he found out he was on a football pitch. He stood up wondering where he was but then he realised he was in the middle of a football match and he had the ball. Then Messi came to the man and said to him, 'You're brilliant, who are you?'

The man said, 'I don't know who I am, I just woke up on this football pitch, where am I?'

Messi said, 'You play for Manchester United.'

The man said, 'I can't believe it.'

Messi said, 'You are Ángel Di María.'

Jake Robinson (10)
St Margaret Mary Catholic Primary School, Carlisle

The Wonderful Life Of Sonny Hull

Once upon a time a young boy called Sonny, who loved playing football, met a beautiful girl named Ariana Grande. Sonny invited her to his house and they got to know each other and so they had a lovely cup of tea from Sonny's mum Jessie J.
Eventually they had a party! After that they went to the village ball and danced all night to the best song ever. Because they were engaged Sonny asked her to marry him, she said yes! So they got married and invited Sonny's friends who were Ronaldo, Messi and Roben.

Sonny Hull (9)
St Margaret Mary Catholic Primary School, Carlisle

The Ice King Of The East

Once upon a time there was a king called Frost, he married a girl called Elsa. They both had ice powers and they covered the whole world in ice. Then everyone shivered until one day Frost lost his powers and then Elsa lost her powers as well because all the ice they had was over the world. Their powers turned into fire powers and they made the winter back to summer. Everyone went to the beach where they'd wanted to go for ages so they were so excited with tears and they jumped in the sea.

Molly Emily Craig (7)
St Margaret Mary Catholic Primary School, Carlisle

Ellis And The Beanstalk

There was a boy called Ellis, he was a very rich man but one day he was sad, he had no money to buy shopping. There was a cow for sale so he bought it. Mum wasn't happy so he sent the cow back and got magic beans. He planted them in the garden.
The next morning there was a big beanstalk so he climbed the beanstalk and found some magic eggs and climbed back down. While he was up there he saw a giant.
Now he was rich so he enjoyed life as a rich man.

Ellis Patrick John Lavery (10)
St Margaret Mary Catholic Primary School, Carlisle

Neo The Huggle Monster's Adventures

Once, there was a huggle monster called Neo. He lived in a poor little shack with no food. He lived with his mum and his pet cow, but sadly needed to sell the cow for food.

So the next day he went to sell the cow at the shop and saw a man who said, 'You want some magic beans for your cow?' When Neo went home he planted the beans. After a day the beans grew into a gigantic beanstalk! It took his breath away! So then he decided to crawl and slide down the beanstalk. It was hell...

Neo Storey (9)
St Margaret Mary Catholic Primary School, Carlisle

Bill's Birthday Adventure

Once there was a snail called Bill who received a letter from his dad saying: 'Come to my house. Be here for 3pm'.
Bill set off to go there, he only had to go through a lake but it was quite eventful. He could not swim or float so he looked around and found a leaf, a stick and used them as a boat. He found a small house. He was sure it was his dad's house but someone almost squashed him! He slithered as fast as he could to get there and when he walked in...
'Happy birthday Bill!'

Charlie Taylor (9)
St Margaret Mary Catholic Primary School, Carlisle

The Polar Bear Who Smashed Ice

Bob was fishing in a chilly country, the North Pole. The lake was as blue as the sky. His shiny fishing rod got trapped in the green weeds. Bob stepped carefully onto the ice, he untangled his rod and started to walk back to land. He didn't notice that the ice had started to crack until he heard a cracking sound coming from under his boots. *Splash!* He had tumbled into the freezing cold water. As he tried to climb out the ice sealed up. Suddenly a polar bear stood on the ice and dragged him out, phew!

Connor Briggs (9)
St Margaret Mary Catholic Primary School, Carlisle

Life Of A Monster

Once there was a monster who'd broken his legs, after that he had to use a wheelchair to get everywhere. Sometimes he would use a lift to get upstairs. Soon he visited the hospital where they gave him tablets to help his legs work.
20 days later he could crawl! Soon he made another visit to the hospital where he found out that he could walk again. So where would he walk now? He visited his mother and she made him some sandwiches. Soon he became a 'Super Monster', he was able to lift ten cars with his arms.

Dylan Hull (10)
St Margaret Mary Catholic Primary School, Carlisle

Football Boy

My father is Ronaldo. He is the best football player ever. By the age of ten I was better than Drogba at football because of Ronaldo, my dad he does personal training with me. Also when he's in a match I can get a VIP seat. They win even against Barcelona. The score is sometimes 4-1 to Real Madrid.
Now I play for Manchester United with Di María, Falcal, Van Persie and Rooney. We've played Arsenal, we won 2-1 but next we have Real Madrid! I know that we're dead!

Mikey Waugh (10)
St Margaret Mary Catholic Primary School, Carlisle

Frozen Part Two

Once upon a time there were four friends, Eridal, Elsa, Anna and Olaf. They were a family. Elsa went into the castle and started to think, *think, think, think.* Then she had an idea. 'I know, I can throw a surprise party for Anna!' So she told Eridal to hide the surprise from her, to just act normal.
A few weeks later it was Anna's birthday, everybody was really happy. Elsa said, 'Anna wake up, it's your birthday!'
Anna jumped up and looked around. 'It's my birthday.' Suddenly she hit Elsa in the face.
'Ouch!' shouted Elsa.
'Sorry!' said Anna.

Kelsey-Lea Clark (11)
St Margaret Mary Catholic Primary School, Carlisle

The Killer Wedding

Once, there was a woman called Clara Bummbleworth. Clara and her brother, Fritz, lived in a three-bedroomed house. Clara was twenty years old and she was getting married to a handsome young prince. Fritz was jealous and never wanted to go to the wedding. A few weeks went and it was Clara's wedding. Everyone was excited except for Fritz. It was time to go to the wedding, Clara looked perfect for the day. When they got there they said their marriage vows. The happy couple got into a limo. They arrived and danced all night and lived happy lives.

Megan Bunting (8)
Scotby CE Primary School, Carlisle

Ocean Adventure

In an ocean far, far, far away was a magical wand that was golden with a diamond at the top. People said it was powerful but only worked for the right person.

Deep in the ocean a mermaid lived. Her name was Lexie. She was no princess but she had beauty, kindness and, of course, a loving heart. But one day she swam, not thinking, and saw the wand. She touched it in fear and suddenly some rocks appeared. She saw with her green eyes they changed colour. She tapped the wand again...

Eva Carthy (8)
Scotby CE Primary School, Carlisle

The Magic Land

Once there was a glittering magical land with an enormous volcano, inside was bubbling lava. Then a hunter called Corn found a land with big mountains and hills. Then, through the year, people started sailing on speed boats and paying a lot of money just to get to a magic land. One misty day the waves were crashing against the magic invisible shield. Suddenly, later that day, the land started to shake. People started yelling, 'What's happening?' Then ash and dust started to fire out of the volcano. As it erupted a superhero saved the day!

Jamie Longrigg (9)
Scotby CE Primary School, Carlisle

Lost In A Magical Land!

Deep in a forest a princess sang a lovely tune. 'I'll soon be queen both strong and caring.' When she came across a deer. The deer spoke. 'Hello,' she continued quietly, 'my name is Caramel.'
'Well I can see why,' but Abby just carried on walking through the forest. She fell down a hole! All she could see were pink trees and bushes that had candyfloss as leaves and giant lollies as flowers. Abby went to explore. While she was walking she found a hot chocolate river. Suddenly she teleported back home.

Katie Blenkinsopp (8)
Scotby CE Primary School, Carlisle

Jake In Space

One morning a small boy named Jake decided to take a walk. He ran to the gloomy park but all of a sudden he stopped to see a dark figure pointing a finger at him. In the blink of an eye he was in deep space. He tried to speak to this alien-like creature. He led Jake to a space tunnel. It was very steep but he just kept going. The alien pointed and Jake wondered if his mum would ever believe him. No one knows about Jake's adventure except Jake and you. No one will ever believe him.

Ellis Beattie (9)
Scotby CE Primary School, Carlisle

Rhubarb's Christmas

It was the first Christmas Eve for squirrel Rhubarb, but it wasn't for Donnie, it was his fifth one. Clever Rhubarb was thinking of a calculation. '5,649.'
'Why don't we just play in the snow?' said Donnie.
'What is snow?'
Then Donnie replied. 'It's a soft kind of...' You could see from Rhubarb's stern looking face he wasn't quite impressed.
After a while, Rhubarb was ready to go outside, he was now filled with happiness! A blizzard was coming in Rhubarb's way but he didn't care. Frightened, Donnie cried out loudly, finally Rhubarb came back in their cosy house.

Daria Nik (9)
Scotby CE Primary School, Carlisle

Flames Under The Sea

One boiling day, under the crystal-clear sea, there lived a young girl called Selena. Selena was a girl who liked to have fun with her friends, so Selena woke up from her cosy bed and ran downstairs and got ready to have fun! Half an hour later, Selena was in the middle of playing tag with her friend. Suddenly, Selena and her friend started to cough. 'It smells like flames,' Selena whispered while looking at her friend. They decided to follow the flames, they ended up in the kitchen! They realised that her mum had left the cooker on.

Sarah-Jane Cochrane (8)
Scotby CE Primary School, Carlisle

Frosty The Snowman

There once was a snowman named Frosty, he lived happily in Snow Land, but it wouldn't last. One day a mysterious figure entered Snow Land, she wore snow-themed clothes, wings, accessories and she held a snowflake staff. Imagine an evil name, hers was Snowla, she took Frosty's pride and joy – his hat. Frosty wouldn't take that, he jumped for his hat but Snowla dodged quickly, however in the process she dropped the black hat and Frosty grabbed it. Snowla went away forever and Frosty ate an ice cream to celebrate and he lived happily forever with his hat.

Caitlan Osgood (10)
Scotby CE Primary School, Carlisle

Christmas In Space!

'Why does Santa never give me a present?' asked Shiver angrily. Shiver was an out of space polar bear. 'I want a present this year!' Two years had passed and Shiver still hadn't got a present. 'This year I am going down to Earth on Christmas Eve and I am going to say why haven't you given me a present?'

That year, on Christmas Eve, Shiver went down and hid behind a massive house. When *whoosh*, a sleigh zoomed past, then landed. 'Hey Shiver,' came a loud booming voice, it was Santa. 'Do you want to have Christmas in space?'

Jessica Anthony (9)
Scotby CE Primary School, Carlisle

Elastico!

This is the biggest game in history! Barcelona Vs Real Madrid, two big players Messi and Ronaldo. Two rivals who both want to win! And we are at the Nou Camp. Messi to Neymar, Iniesta makes a run, he shoots and it's in! Iniesta is the scorer! We are off again, Ronaldo passes to one and another, Neymar shoots, deflects off Xavi and it is in, and in the 89th minutes. And we are off again. Messi scores in the 90th minute. One minute left, Messi shoots and it's in! Full time.

Sam Glencross (8)
Scotby CE Primary School, Carlisle

What Do Teachers Do In The Staffroom?

Want to know what happens in the staffroom? Well, I will tell you. This is when the teachers play Rock Guitar and play with all the toys that they've banned and confiscated. And all the mean teachers become kind and all the kind teachers become mean, and fight over toys! And when they say, 'I am going for a cup of tea,' they're actually going to play on a computer. At break they watch TV and play video games. They never let you in in case you play on their games!

Oliver Kennedy (9)
Scotby CE Primary School, Carlisle

The Christmas Wish

It was Christmas Eve, Jake was extremely excited. He really
wanted a skateboard, sweets and he kept on imagining all
that chocolate he wanted. He really liked Galaxy but he loved
Cadbury's.
It was nearly bedtime, 8.30pm, Jake went to sleep. Santa came
but he had a nightmare that Santa didn't come and eat all the
mince pies and the tasty milk. He woke up, it was Christmas Day!
He went to his nana's on Christmas Day, when he came back and
opened his presents, he got what he wanted – all the chocolate
and sweets!

Charlotte Bell (9)
Scotby CE Primary School, Carlisle

Imagine What Your Teddies Do At Night

Imagine what your teddies do at night. Do they eat all your cookies or drink all your milk? They might jump on your bed or even wake you up. They might even watch TV. We wish we could see what they do!

However, one night, out of my left eye, I saw something amazing, my teddies were dancing and drinking Coke! They beckoned me to join in so I did, but I was up most of the night. I'm not a morning person (groan), I'm glad it was the holidays. I guess my story has come to an end, bye!

Olivia Robertson (10)
Scotby CE Primary School, Carlisle

A Trip To The Moon

There was a girl called Sally, Kate was her sister, her dad had died, so she only had her mum. Sally and Kate had a dream to fly to the moon! When they were grown up they lived their dream. Sally and Kate got into their suit and jumped into the rocket. 5! 4! 3! 2! 1! They shot right up higher and higher. Soon they could see every planet in space. Suddenly, they spotted a green alien! Somehow, they weren't afraid! Kate and Sally had tears of joy in their eyes. They had finally completed their dream.

Holly Robins (9)
Scotby CE Primary School, Carlisle

Clash Of Clan Double Trouble

One ordinary day a boy called Tom was playing his new game he had just downloaded on his iPod. He wondered what it would be like to be one of those characters, maybe a barbarian or an archer. It was late now and he had to go to bed. He woke up tired, his eyes flickered and saw a yellow-haired man just like the barbarian in his game! There was two – double trouble! Soon his mum was coming up the stairs. He shoved them in a cupboard. A lucky escape? Argh, maybe not! Dang!

Joseph Grayson (9)
Scotby CE Primary School, Carlisle

The Royal Puppy

Long, long ago there once lived a princess puppy. It became winter and snow fell and there was ice all over the ground. Shiver got lost and she was far away from home. The queen sent requests to all of the guards to find the royal puppy and she said the puppy was in the garden, because it was snowing, maybe she'd sank into it. The guards all split up and one fell and slipped but found the puppy and returned it home safely, the queen said, 'Hello Shiver,' and they lived happily.

Poppi Bowe (9)
Scotby CE Primary School, Carlisle

Dragon Danger!

Joel quickly crept up to his pet dragon who was sleeping. He was called Thunderslash and he was purple with spikes. Joel removed his leash and they went flying over Hyrule. Suddenly, a Firewing started attacking the village's food storage. Joel and Thunderslash decided to distract Firewing to save the food. They led it away from the village towards the sea. They dived into the water so when the Firewing followed its wings were damaged. It couldn't fly anymore. The food was saved! But Joel didn't realise there was worse to come. An even more dangerous dragon was approaching!

Joel McCormick (7)
Scotby CE Primary School, Carlisle

My Unusual Mission

I was very excited. I looked out of the window and I could see my destination. I was zooming towards an unknown planet. It took a long time to get there. When I stepped out of my rocket I saw a weird creature with a hover board instead of legs. He was friendly and took me to his home. His friend's hover board was broken so he needed me to fix it. Luckily I had just the right tools. It took a very long time but finally I fixed it! They were very happy so I said goodbye and returned.

Matthew Bell (7)
Scotby CE Primary School, Carlisle

The Amazing Romans

I was walking on the beach when I tripped and fell down, down, down. When I woke up it looked like I was on a battlefield. Then I realised I was on a Roman battlefield. I didn't know how to get home but I really wanted to. Suddenly I could hear the sound of footsteps marching closer and closer. I could see men carrying huge, heavy shields. I was terrified. I started to run in the opposite direction but I tripped and fell down, down, down. I found myself back on the beach. Was it a dream? Maybe, maybe not!

Rae Platton (7)
Scotby CE Primary School, Carlisle

A Suspicious Week!

A strange thing happened. An elf and a fairy came to my house. They were very naughty. They kept coming to wreck my bedroom. So one day I stayed up until they came to my house again. Then I said to them, 'Please could you stop it?' But they just ignored me. So I had to shout. Then they listened to me. But they said, 'No!' I didn't know what to do.

But the next day, they came to me and said, 'We will stop wrecking your bedroom if you don't shout at us.'

So I said, 'OK, I won't.'

Rosie Cairns (7)
Scotby CE Primary School, Carlisle

An Unspecial Adventure

An amazing thing happened to me. I was strolling along the beach when suddenly I tripped on a rock and fell down, down, down. When I woke up I realised I had a mermaid tail! Then I heard a quiet voice. It was a beautiful mermaid. Her name was Ella and she was very kind. She took me to her underwater world. I saw colourful fish and we made pearl tiaras. We even had clams for snacks. Later I fell asleep but when I woke up I was on the beach again. I was soaking wet. Was it a dream?

Cerys Richardson (7)
Scotby CE Primary School, Carlisle

Why I Didn't Get Any Presents

I opened my eyes and stretched, then suddenly remembered that it was Christmas Day! I jumped up and looked in my stocking, but there was nothing there! Then I remembered I had been naughty. What could I do? I could start being good! So I made breakfast, washed the dishes and even emptied the bin.

Later on, when Granny fell in the snow, I gave first aid. That night I had another look in my stocking and there was a present! But I was so tired after being good all day. I fell asleep before I could open it!

Dylan Nettleship (7)
Scotby CE Primary School, Carlisle

Haunted House

It was pitch-black. Everything was quiet except for the leaves rustling in the trees. I called for my mum but she was nowhere to be found. I thought for a minute, then I decided to go in the building. I screamed when a spider appeared from the darkness. Suddenly, I saw someone. She was wearing a black cape and a pointy hat. She came closer. I was horrified. She pointed her bony finger with a sharp nail towards me. I was terrified. Then she turned and switched on the light. I couldn't believe it. It was my mum!

Ella Smith (7)
Scotby CE Primary School, Carlisle

The Amazing Trip To Space

James looked out of the window. The stars were shining brightly in the pitch-black sky. In the distance he saw an unusual planet. He steered his rocket towards it. The rocket landed with a bang. He stepped out, but he couldn't see anything except the rocky ground. Suddenly, a strange green creature appeared from behind a massive rock. James was scared. But the creature said, 'Come and get some food.' It was a really friendly alien! So James followed it to its home. He had some delicious food then he jumped back into his rocket and blasted off.

Ethan Bell (7)
Scotby CE Primary School, Carlisle

Me And Santa

It was snowing. All of a sudden I heard a sound behind a tree. I crept towards it and I saw a man. I also saw a reindeer with a red nose. I said to myself, 'Is that Rudolph?' I peeked behind the tree. It was Santa Claus! I saw his sleigh and all the reindeer. He took me to his workshop. He asked me to make some toys – it was a disaster! Luckily his elves were doing a better job. When the presents were finished he took me on his sleigh to my house then delivered all the presents.

Jasmine Murray (7)
Scotby CE Primary School, Carlisle

Lost

One sunny day Stella and her twin sister Bella went to the beach with their mum. 'Come on Stella, let's go for a swim in the sea!' yelled Bella.
So they went for a paddle, then they decided to go and play a game of hide-and-seek.
'Go hide and I'll count!' explained Stella, so Bella hid! Stella counted to 100 and went to find her sister. She fell down a hole and couldn't get out! A long time passed. She went to look for Stella.
'Help!' Stella yelled.
'There you are!' Bella said happily.
So they went home!

Petrina Walker (10)
Scotby CE Primary School, Carlisle

The Dirty Baker

'Run, run as fast as you can, you can't catch me I'm the biscuit
man!'
There were bakers, teachers, doctors, foxes, all chasing the biscuit
man for different reasons. You see the biscuit man has strange
ingredients in his biscuits. He stole sausages from the butchers,
snot from the doctors, rulers from the teachers and hairs from the
foxes. He's on Santa's naughty list! I wouldn't want to eat one of his
biscuits, yuck! Also he doesn't wash his hands before baking the
biscuits.
But luckily, they caught him, slapped him and threw him in the
pond!

Charlie Lomas
Scotby CE Primary School, Carlisle

The Bank Job

One day there was an evil hippo who loved robbing banks. His next job was one of the biggest banks in Europe. He was going to rob Halifax. He couldn't stop thinking about all the money he would get, little did he know who guarded it, he'd regret it... Super Monkey guarded it, he is the best guard in the world. That evening Evil Hippo snuck up and went through the open window. Super Monkey was inside the vault so he'd attack anyone who opened the door. Evil Hippo opened the vault door *bang!* He would never rob again!

Sam Jamieson (10)
Scotby CE Primary School, Carlisle

The Deadly Peas

When the shoppers put their hands in the freezer to get peas for dinner, the peas fight for their lives not to be eaten. When people try to get a bag of frozen peas, the peas have got a pea machine gun so they poke their eyes with the peas from the gun and they pull the people in and freeze them for the whole night until they forget who they are.

One day a man came to get some peas but the peas were asleep and he took the bag of peas home to eat with pie!

Liam Robinson (10)
Scotby CE Primary School, Carlisle

Trixie's Sea Treasure

Yesterday we were at the seaside. Me, Trixie and Jessie were sunbathing. Rex, Kittysaurus and Mr Pork Chop were in the rock pools. Suddenly Kittysaurus fell down all the rock pools into the sea. I was brave enough to hold my breath for longer than five minutes and save her. I tied a rope around my waist and dived in after her. The rope snapped so I grabbed Kittysaurus and swam up. That's how I enjoyed my playtime, with only a paddling pool and cardboard boxes!

Robyn Bainbridge (11)
Scotby CE Primary School, Carlisle

The Toy Robot Predicament

There I was standing in the middle of my destroyed garage, holding
a blowtorch and hammer with a toy robot. Here's how it began. I
woke up one morning and ate my breakfast. I thought it would be
a good idea to modify my robot. I took it into the garage, took out
some of my dad's tools, took off the exhaust pipe from the car and
started hammering it onto my robot. Then I heard a rumbling sound
coming from the car. Suddenly it exploded and took the garage roof
with it. And that's how the story began.

Jacob Platton (11)
Scotby CE Primary School, Carlisle

The Stairs

When I was three I was dressing up with princess high heels, a dolly pram with a doll. I walked downstairs to show my nana. As I took the first step I fell. My sister laughed at me and my nana told me to come over and she put a wet cloth on my arm because it hurt. When my mum came back, she got told the story. So, anyway, we all went camping and when I lay on my arm I cried. After two weeks, Mum took me to the hospital and found out my wrist was broken.

Leah Barnes (10)
Scotby CE Primary School, Carlisle

You Must Believe

When I was little I used to think that if you believed that you could turn into anything that you want, it would happen. At school I tried to turn into a book but it didn't work so I tried to turn into a pool and it didn't work so I told my teacher, he wished that he was a worm and it finally worked. So all my friends laughed. Emily threw the worm (which was my teacher) out the window, a bird came, found and took it and my teacher has never ever been seen since!

Ellie Swift (10)
Scotby CE Primary School, Carlisle

Paintballing

'Argh!' screamed Alex when Finn shot him in the butt. Alex got revenge and shot Finn in the back so Finn ran to the tree walk and climbed the ladder to fire at Alex. Alex saw him though and did rapid fire and Finn nearly fell but Finn regained his balance and ran along the walk firing all the time and then he jumped down, shot Alex in the leg, making him fall over. Finn ran over to Alex and bent over and put the muzzle of the paintball gun to Alex's butt and said, 'Who's won now?' and shot!

Finlay Barraclough (9)
Scotby CE Primary School, Carlisle

The Three Polar Bears And A Snowman

One freezing, icy-cold day there were three polar bears and there was one snowman. Then one day the three polar bears went out for a big walk in the gigantic woods and the big, fat, lazy snowman went walking into the three big bears' house. He tried Daddy's Christmas dinner but it was too hot so he tried Mummy's Christmas dinner but it was too cold, so he ran to Baby Bear's Christmas dinner and tried his and it was just right, so he ate it all up! Then suddenly, he saw the polar bears walking back... oh no!

Eve Cogan (9)
Scotby CE Primary School, Carlisle

I Can Fly! Not!

When I was young I used to think a lot of things, one of them was I thought I could fly. I used to jump off chairs and fall flat on my face, but one day it happened, I flew! It started at school, I was standing on the concrete stairs, I took a leap and I did it! I shouted out, 'I am a flying human!' But sadly, it was just a dream, and I woke everyone in the house up with my crazy shouting. This story will stay with me forever and ever.

Abbie Kenny (10)
Scotby CE Primary School, Carlisle

The Great Journey

On a cold, snowy night I was going to Cornwall on holiday. I decided to go on a ship to explore. My mum and dad came too and my brother, who is really annoying. Terribly, on the ship, I got lost, I was very scared. So I went down the stairs and found a monkey and tiger. When I was going to see them up close a gigantic wave came and flooded the ship. I saw a boat so I quickly grabbed it and jumped overboard with the cheeky monkey, but the terrible tiger followed, it was scary.

Sophie Irving (9)
Scotby CE Primary School, Carlisle

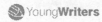
Untitled

One horrible day aliens were invading, that's right – aliens! There was one man that could save us, that was Louis Walsh. It was all because Simon Cowell had been kidnapped so Louie ripped off his sleeves and wrapped a cloth around his head and ran off the building he was standing on and jumped on the massive shuttle. He silently smashed through the window and popped his head around the corner. He saw Simon about to be stabbed by the aliens so knew he had to save him. He ran and barged past them and saved the day, again!

Matthew Walker Scott (11)
Scotby CE Primary School, Carlisle

General Grumpyface
Saves The Martians!

The Martians from Jupiter were under attack. General Grumpyface received the message and set to work getting to Jupiter, the planet – *not* the Roman god! Then, with the help of some troops and poisonous gas-filled balloon guns, General Grumpyface defeated the half-cow, human creatures and saved the Martians! After that the Martians from Jupiter – bit strange, they should be from Mars but that's how it goes – gave General Grumpyface and his troops a feast to remember and some dance moves too! Because Martians are so nice, they also gave him some weaponry and a smiley face mask! Perfect!

Maddie Wildridge (10)
Scotby CE Primary School, Carlisle

One Cold Winter Day

At the very beginning of a cold and frosty December, Walter aged twenty-one (my grandad) was fighting in the royal navy. He saved a ship full of wheat from being sunk by the Germans. Walter sailed alongside the huge metal vessel and kept his trusty gun aimed and ready poised to fire. When the German soldiers tried to board the boat Walter, brave as a lion, fought twenty fierce and ferocious German solders. Thanks to lovely Grandad we got the wheat through to make our daily bread. The crew was decorated for their great bravery, it was never forgotten.

Keira Perrett (10)
The Bishop Harvey Goodwin School (Church Of England Voluntary Aided), Carlisle

Tragic WWI

Trevor went to the army. He was stuck in the trenches. They used war tanks. Trevor was a sniper. After that, Trevor got put on the front line. Trevor was a really good sniper. Then Trevor was put in no-man's-land. All of his family were missing him. Then Trevor got captured by one of the Germans. The Germans were starting to attack from the front line. Germany were speeding to the front line. Then Trevor escaped. All of the trenches were full with Germans and British soldiers. Then the UK won the war.

Kyle McNeill (10)
The Bishop Harvey Goodwin School (Church Of England Voluntary Aided), Carlisle

That Frosty Morning!

It was a cold, frosty morning in the headquarters. Me and the other soldiers were getting trained for the battle against Germany. There was a boy called Jeff who was a bit nervous to battle with Germany for the first time. Two hours before the war began James was messing around, however the other soldiers were getting annoyed with him! Once the war began it was harder than we thought but, sadly, during the battle my brother Benny died because of Scarlet Fever. Me and the other soldiers got upset because of Benny dying. RIP Benny.

Maisie Little (10)
The Bishop Harvey Goodwin School (Church Of England Voluntary Aided), Carlisle

Elf

One day there was a tall elf. But how did he grow big? Well that's the thing. He didn't like being big. So one day he asked Santa Claus to change him back to normal. You would have thought that he liked being big but he didn't because the other elves were making a joke out of him. It wasn't funny but Santa had a plan. His plan was to make a potion to shrink him back to normal size, Elf didn't like that plan but he tried it and it worked so Elf was extremely pleased!

Candice O'Neil (9)
The Bishop Harvey Goodwin School (Church Of England Voluntary Aided), Carlisle

Santa Spies

Once upon a time there lived three children called Rose, Candice and Gemma. They were desperate to find Santa. They waited a whole year for Christmas to see him. They were getting excited about Christmas. How could they find Santa Claus?
Then Christmas Eve came and they were on a mission. They had everything set up to see Santa. There he was! They'd found him! They took a picture of him then he just vanished.

Ellie Troughton (9)
The Bishop Harvey Goodwin School (Church Of England Voluntary Aided), Carlisle

Football Fever

One day a boy was born, he was in love with football. As soon as he started school he was in the school football team and he joined Carlisle football team, his life was all about football. The time flew by and when he left school he got a huge opportunity – to play for England. He accepted the offer but one day, when he was in the squad, he did not know what to do, it was like he'd lost his memory! Suddenly he got a bad hack, then he remembered what to do, then he was the best

Melissa Russell (10)
The Bishop Harvey Goodwin School (Church Of England Voluntary Aided), Carlisle

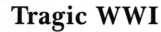

Tragic WWI

On Christmas Eve 1914 Walter joined the army. He got stuck in the trenches. Walter had a friend called Jessie. Walter's brother is called Ben. Ben had to go into no-man's-land to put up barbed wire, he got blown up. Walter was a sniper and a medic. Walter had another friend called Kyle. In the first three days Jessie was shot and killed. When Walter was sniping he didn't realise that a German had thrown a grenade and blew up Kyle. Walter went to see what happened then a German shot him, he died.

Oliver Jessiman (11)
The Bishop Harvey Goodwin School (Church Of England Voluntary Aided), Carlisle

The Long Wait

A boy wakes up, it's the first of December, he had a long wait until the twenty-fifth. He spins on a chair. One glance at the clock, time moves slowly. On the second day he stares out of the window, time moves slowly.

Twenty-three long days pass; on Christmas Eve he gobbles his dinner. He goes to sleep in the hope that Christmas will come quickly.

On Christmas Day, he woke and gave a present to his parents. They smiled at him. They were so happy to have their present, they gave him a hug. He was so happy!

Rebecca Bevins (10)
The Bishop Harvey Goodwin School (Church Of England Voluntary Aided), Carlisle

Penguin's Jobs

Once there was a penguin called Travis Bennett, he liked to stay in the house to do some jobs. One time Travis the penguin had to go to the shop but he would not go to the shop. Then he had an idea, so he went on the Internet to shop online. The next day the shopping was not there so Travis went out to the store to get the shopping. Then Travis went to the top counter and said, 'Where's my shopping?'
'It's OK, I will get it.'
When Travis got back to his home it was on fire!

Travis Bennett (9)
The Bishop Harvey Goodwin School (Church Of England Voluntary Aided), Carlisle

The Football Of WWI

There was a team, Yogi Park Whites. We were named after our manager (Yogi Ronaldo) who also owned the stadium called Yanky Pie! This was their squad: Henry Banboosher followed by Jessy Burn, Jack Felini and their captain Guss Nicholson. We were the best team ever. Beating Barcelona 3-1 and PSG 1-0. But now for the final! Real Madrid! We began to panic a lot. We had seen all of their matches. They beat Chelsea 7-0 and Barcelona 4-0! But we won 4-3! Our manager passed out in excitement!

Ethan Nicholson (10)
The Bishop Harvey Goodwin School (Church Of England Voluntary Aided), Carlisle

WWI

One frosty morning there was a man called Apil. He was a spy who had to collect information for the Germans. He was on the German's side, he needed to pretend to be on Britain's side so he could get information. Apil went to ask the general, 'When are we going to the trenches?'
He said, 'Tomorrow.'
Apil got to the trenches and he received a package from his wife. It had photos, food and clothes in. He was frightened and he died. He was remembered by his family.

Jacob Callaghan (10)
The Bishop Harvey Goodwin School (Church Of England Voluntary Aided), Carlisle

The Angel That Came Into My Life

Once a girl called Serena had a dog called Tango who was very naughty. Eventually Serena's mum decided that Tango had to be replaced with a good dog called Freya. Unfortunately, a few days later Tango came back for vengeance. Tango chased after Freya but Freya was too fast and got back to the family just on time so they could drive away. They got home and cuddled their angelic dog and Serena and Freya played together all night long. As for Tango, she was never to be seen again!

Serena Cooper (8)
Windermere Preparatory School, Windermere

YoungWriters

The Story Of Bow And Arrow

Once upon a time there lived two children called Bow and Arrow.
They grew up in a forest, they wanted to go to the city but Ladues
and his army of lizards stopped them. One day the two children
went exploring but got trapped and got taken to the Castle of
Terror. That is where Ladues lived. They were trapped for days.
One day they escaped and found a city and lived happily ever after.

Hector Westmoreland Nicholson (8)
Windermere Preparatory School, Windermere

Santa In Space

One day, on Christmas Eve, Santa was travelling to the 56,000th person. Suddenly the sleigh flew directly into space! Santa put his air tank on, then Santa saw what looked like Mrs Claus flying on Rudolph because he was spare this year. It was Mrs Claus, she hooked Rudolph onto the chassis with some of the elves' sticky tape. The Rudolph started running faster and faster then Rudolph suddenly stood very, very still, then Santa pulled at the reins but it didn't work. Would everybody get their presents delivered by Santa?

Josh Done (8)
Windermere Preparatory School, Windermere

The Elf Who Saved Christmas

Once upon a time, an elf was wrapping presents. It was so exciting because it was almost Christmas. It was Christmas Eve! He was busy wrapping parcels when, in came an elf dressed in black, who began unwrapping the presents! When he had finished, the good elf went to Santa and told him that the bad elf had unwrapped the gifts. Fortunately, Santa used some of his magic to rewrap the presents before setting off to deliver them to all the girls and boys around the world. 'Merry Christmas,' he roared as he waved goodbye to all the elves.

Emma Heginbotham (9)
Windermere Preparatory School, Windermere

Stolen Husky

Once there lived a small husky named Pip and her owner Maisie. Pip liked where she lived. She liked looking at the Northern Lights. One day they entered a little hut. Maisie went to the fire to keep warm but Pip spied a glowing circle, she stepped in it, suddenly she went into a world which was too cold for her. Then she got grabbed by a polar bear. She tried to get away but couldn't. Later she crept across the snow, avoided the polar bear and got out and scampered back home.

Eva Baker (8)
Windermere Preparatory School, Windermere

Presents

Once there was an elf called Spencer. He wrapped all of Santa's presents. But when Spencer went on holiday, Santa had a problem because he didn't know how to wrap presents. He needed to find someone who could do the job. He took off his red coat and put on some pyjamas as a disguise.

Ten days later, Santa had looked everywhere and decided that nobody else would do so he jumped on an aeroplane to Australia. He found Elf and begged him to come home. Spencer returned with Santa and wrapped all the presents just in time.

Charlie Hodson (8)
Windermere Preparatory School, Windermere

The Two Boys And The Army

Once upon a time there were two boys that saw a giant island in the distance. John and Joe wanted to go there. John and Joe went to it and entered it. When they entered it they saw a giant army. The army was made of scorpions. The army charged at John and Joe. John and Joe ran for their lives into a big, dark forest. The forest was really scary. John and Joe went back and sneaked past the army and saw it standing there and the army said goodbye. After that John and Joe went back home successfully.

Cristian Waddell Lallana (8)
Windermere Preparatory School, Windermere

Untitled

One day a girl called Rosie wanted a dog but one night she had an amazing idea, she was going to escape to the North Pole. Surely Santa had a dog.
The next few days she spent planning an escape plan to the North Pole.
The next day, she finally got to the North Pole and she looked around and saw Santa and he had two puppies with him. She walked to Santa and he gave her a husky then Santa gave her a ride home on his sleigh. When she got home she went on adventures with her husky.

Clarissa Cooper (9)
Windermere Preparatory School, Windermere

The Nasty Elf And
The Clever Child

One day a nasty elf wanted to destroy a village, but a clever
little girl got in her way. The village was a lovely, beautiful place,
everyone had lots and lots of fun there. One day the elf attempted
to blow up the village but the little girl got in her way. The next day
the little girl tried to blow up the elf. She didn't manage to but the elf
ran away and everyone lived happily ever after.

Elizabeth Kaye (8)
Windermere Preparatory School, Windermere

What I Realised

One day I was playing in the pretty park with my friends, when I felt left out and very lonely. I wandered off in search of fun. Just then, a sparkle of light appeared out of nowhere. It said, 'Let me show you what life would be like without you.' So I walked into the light to see for myself. I soon realised I was important in the world and I lived happily ever after with my friends. I never felt unimportant again.

Bethany Saunders (9)
Windermere Preparatory School, Windermere

The Rose Fairy

Once there was a child called Charlotte. Everybody thought she was ordinary but looking over her shoulder was a tiny rose fairy. Charlotte was unaware of her small friend. As she got older Charlotte grew more beautiful but one cursed day Charlotte felt unwell. The rose fairy flew her to the beautiful rose garden where she picked up a rose and sprinkled the petals over her. Charlotte began to feel better and noticed the rose fairy. She was so scared but the rose fairy gave her a smile and they remained friends for evermore.

Katie Holgate (8)
Windermere Preparatory School, Windermere

The Diamond Box

Once, a boy called Galaxy was bored, he decided to go outside to look for something. After 30 minutes he went in, but on the decking he saw a diamond-shaped box. He remembered seeing the shape in a wall, so he went in, found the wall and put it in. Suddenly a portal shot out! Galaxy went in, found himself in an enchanted forest where he met me, Gomez. The world he was in was amazing. When Swampy, his arch-enemy, was shooting paralyser at us, Galaxy put lemonade in Swampy's water tank and Swampy could not breathe!

Hamish Ross (8)
Windermere Preparatory School, Windermere

The Doctor And Santa

Once, in the freezing North Pole lived Santa! It was nearly Christmas Eve and the elves were hard at work making wonderful gifts. Santa was also working hard checking his list. Finally they were ready! Santa was in his Christmas sleigh! Then he set off on his way to China. Santa was injected by an evil doctor! Santa forgot what to do and started delivering garbage from all the bins in town. It was terribly bad. An elf knew he had to kill Santa's wife to change him back. But! Magically Santa's wife came back to life!

Eddie Lewis (8)
Windermere Preparatory School, Windermere

Santa's Problem

Santa Claus once was delivering presents to the little children but then he suddenly noticed that everybody had forgotten all about Christmas so then Santa came up with an idea. His idea was to bring back Christmas. Santa told everybody to meet under the Christmas tree in the middle of town. So everybody gathered around the Christmas tree and everybody was wondering what was going to happen. But suddenly Santa started to count down from 30 and then suddenly all of the Christmas lights turned on and then a few minutes later the Christmas spirit was back!

Taya Wade-Wilson (8)
Windermere Preparatory School, Windermere

No Presents

Santa doesn't deliver any exciting presents this year. So Sam wanted to find out why. Sam quickly dashed into the clean kitchen. He got some yummy food for the long journey, he was going to the freezing North Pole to help Santa! Next he got onto a colossal plane. When he got there he helped Santa load the massive presents. After a few tiring hours he went to his warm home. The presents were a bit late anyway but Sam lived happily ever after.

Tom Johnson (8)
Windermere Preparatory School, Windermere

A Trip To The Moon

Once upon a time me, Jake and Ranulph went on a trip to the moon but... we got pulled in by a worm hole! It pulled us into another galaxy where we saw a miniscule planet and landed on it. There we met some aliens called Bob, Steve, Dave, Kyle and Jack, his sidekick, but they could not catch us. We hopped into our shiny new powered rocket and, in a millisecond, it soared out of orbit. In a minute I was home safe from aliens or anything dangerous.

Felix Hugo Stewart (7)
Windermere Preparatory School, Windermere

My Big Fairy Adventure

One day I went to the bottom of the garden and found a potion. There I saw a weeny door. I thought about what the potion would do, so I drank it and went through the weeny door. At first I struggled to fit through the door but then I managed to fit. Then I met a seal on the edge of a pool and went in the wood. I looked at my watch. It was five o'clock back home, so I saw a cookie, ate it, got big and I went home.

Harriet Read (7)
Windermere Preparatory School, Windermere

A Trip To The North Pole With Santa

Once upon a time there was a little girl called Petal and her dream was to go on Santa's sleigh with Rudolph. One cold, frosty and foggy night on Christmas Eve, Santa came and took Petal with him, he was a jolly old chap with a nose like a cherry. She got on the sleigh. When she got to the North Pole she couldn't believe her eyes, there was snow everywhere, so she ended up staying there and said goodbye to her mum and dad.

Patia May Pickering (8)
Windermere Preparatory School, Windermere

The Story Of Me And Mark

This Christmas I was getting the Christmas decorations from the attic. I met a bear. He said he was called Mark. I gave Mark a warm cup of tea. We discussed our totally different lives. Afterwards he offered to help decorate the tree. But first I gave him a tour of my house. When I asked him to put the angel on top he went up the stepladder and toppled over! At long last it got dark, Mark climbed up to the attic. I went to sleep, dreaming happily.

Nuala Sankey (8)
Windermere Preparatory School, Windermere

Untitled

A little girl sailed across the seven seas and suddenly Lilly saw a big island covered in horses. *It's cool,* she thought. She got off the boat and swam to the beach on the island and afterwards she found a beautiful horse with a pink strip of mane. Lilly said, 'She's beautiful. I'm going for this one, I like her, I'm calling her Majesty.' Soon she took Lilly to a place with more of these strange ponies, it was fascinating and they lived happily ever after.

Millie Westmoreland Nicholson (7)
Windermere Preparatory School, Windermere

Bob And Boo

There was a man called Bob. He liked spaceships. He was getting into a rocket. He was excited. He got to the moon and saw an alien. The alien spoke English. He had six noses, one eye and three mouths. Then they played lots of games. They both got in the rocket. Bob named him Boo. They got home. Bob made Boo's bed. They were very tired after their adventure.

Jake Harris (8)
Windermere Preparatory School, Windermere

Castle Building

Once upon a time I saw a broken castle. 'I have an idea, let's rebuild it so we have a home to live in.' We built a village inside it, and there was a war.
'Let's go to the blacksmith to get tools and weapons to use in battles.' We protected our castle.
'Tonight we will keep guard of the castle from our enemies who will attack our castle... Oh no! Enemies are attacking! Soldiers attack the enemies!'

Ranulph Turton (7)
Windermere Preparatory School, Windermere

Evil Santa!

Santa was whizzing round one day when the posh sleigh went zooming into a bush, then Santa fell straight into the freezing cold snow. Suddenly the massive sleigh slowly went into the dark cave. A couple of hours later John, the elf, found him shivering in the ice-cold snow. After Santa got up John said, 'What happened?' 'Nothing,' replied Santa with a rather croaky voice. Next they went into the black cave. They saw a dim light in the far distance, they followed the light and found a person with a black beard.

Tom Johnson (8)
Windermere Preparatory School, Windermere

YOUNG WRITERS INFORMATION

We hope you have enjoyed reading this book – and that you will continue to in the coming years.

If you're a young writer who enjoys reading and creative writing, or the parent of an enthusiastic poet or story writer, do visit our website www.youngwriters.co.uk. Here you will find free competitions, workshops and games, as well as recommended reads, a poetry glossary and our blog.

If you would like to order further copies of this book, or any of our other titles, give us a call or visit **www.youngwriters.co.uk.**

Young Writers, Remus House
Coltsfoot Drive, Peterborough, PE2 9BF

(01733) 890066 / 898110
info@youngwriters.co.uk